Chinese Tale Series

中国神话

Jingwei Filling the Sea

精卫填海

Adapted and Illustrated by
Feng jiannan

据中国古代神话

冯健男　改编绘画

Dolphin Books

海豚出版社　北京

First Edition 1991

一九九·年　第一版

Hardcover: ISBN 0-8351-2727-3　ISBN 7-80051-681-4
Paperback: ISBN 0-8351-2728-1　ISBN 7-80051-682-2

Copyright 1991 by Dolphin Books,Beijing, China

Published by Dolphin Books
24 Baiwanzhuang Road, Beijing 100037, China

Distributed by China International Book Trading
Corporation
21 Chegongzhuang Xilu, Beijing 100044, China
P.O. Box 399, Beijing, China

Printed in the People's Republic of China

在中华人民共和国印刷

Legend has it that the Great Emperor Yan had three beautiful and kind daughters.

相传大神炎帝有三个女儿，她们长得都非常美丽，而且善良。

The eldest daughter was a skilled farmer. She could do almost all kinds of farm work.

大女儿是个种庄稼的能手,耕耘播种,她样样都行。

The second daughter was Yaoji. She collected herbs and concocted medicine to help people who suffered from disease.

二女儿叫瑶姬。她尝草制药，为民治病解痛。

The youngest daughter, Nüwa, was extremely brave and strong-willed.

三女儿叫女娃。她特别勇敢、坚强。

One day, Nüwa went to the East Sea and was fascinated by the colourful shells on the beach.

一天，女娲来到东海，被海滩上那些五光十色的贝壳吸引住了。

She picked up shells as she walked along the beach. Before she knew it, she had already walked into the sea.

她边走边拾贝壳，不知不觉走进了海水里。

When she saw the sea birds flying freely in the sky and the fish swimming leisurely in the sea, she felt very envious.

当她看到在空中自由飞翔的海鸟、水里畅游的鱼儿时,心里无比羡慕。

She thought to herself, "It would be wonderful if people could not only walk on earth, but also fly in the sky and swim in the water!"

女娲想：人要是既能在地上走，又能在天上飞，也能在水里游，那该多好哇。

She was lost in her thoughts. Suddenly, she saw a beautiful palace emerging from the horizon.

她想着想着，突然看见大海的不远处出现了一座美丽的宫殿。

She got into a boat and rowed towards the palace.

她坐上一只小船，很快地向那座宫殿划去。

She rowed and rowed. The sun was setting. She still had not reached the palace.

她划呀,划呀,一直划到太阳快落山了,却还没能划到那座宫殿跟前。

Night fell. Nüwa was exhausted. But she still kept rowing.

夜幕降临了，女娃又饿又累。为了达到目的，她坚持向前划着。

The sky was very dark. Stars were twinkling at her. Under the shining moonlight, she rowed towards the palace with all her might.

夜深了,天上的星星对她眨着眼睛,她借着银色的月光,奋力向宫殿划去。

Suddenly, she heard a splash. The water in front of her boat became rough. The Sea Dragon King appeared.

忽然，一阵水响，小船前面的海水波浪滔天，原来是海龙王来了。

"Hey!" shouted the Sea Dragon King angrily. "Rowing at this time of night, you woke me up from my beautiful dream! Get back immediately!"

海龙王很不高兴地对女娃嚷着:"喂! 你半夜三更在这儿划船,把我的美梦都打碎啦,快将小船划回去!"

"I'm sorry, Dragon King," said Nüwa politely. "I want to go to the palace and have a look."

女娃很有礼貌地回答说:"对不起,老龙王,我要划到前面的宫殿去看看。"

When the Sea Dragon King saw the Nüwa wouldn't go back, he blew at the water. All of a sudden, the smooth sea surged violently.

海龙王见女娃不肯划回去,便对海水轻轻地吹了一口气,原来风平浪静的海面霎时波涛汹涌。

The small boat tossed about like a leaf in the sea. Yet Nüwa didn't show any fear. She rowed on with all her strength

这时，小船就像一片树叶似的在海浪里上下地颠簸着，可是女娲却毫无惧色地用力划船。

After a little while, the Sea Dragon King appeared again in front of the boat, blocking her way. "If you don't go back, you'll be sorry!"

过了一会儿，海龙王又站到女娃的小船前面拦住去路，气势汹汹地说："如果你再不把船划回去，我就对你不客气了！"

Seeing that the Sea Dragon King was so rude, Nüwa dashed her boat right at him.

女娃看见海龙王这样蛮不讲理,便奋力将小船向他撞去。

The Sea Dragon King was unprepared and he fell. He was enraged.

海龙王毫无防备,竟被小船撞倒了。他气得大发雷霆。

In the twinkling of an eye, a wild wind started to blow and dark clouds started to roll. Row after row of waves as huge as small mountains attacked Nüwa and her small boat.

眨眼间,海上狂风大作,空中乌云翻滚;一排排巨浪像一座座小山似的向女娃和小船压来。

Nüwa and her boat were at one moment tossed by the waves up to the sky, and the next thrown into the sea.

女娲和小船一会儿被巨浪抛到天上，一会儿又被甩跌到浪下。

Suddenly, the boat ran up on a rock and broke into pieces.

突然，小船撞到一块大礁石上。小船被撞碎了。

Holding onto a piece of board, Nüwa struggled in the sea.

女娃抱着一块木板拼命地在风浪里游着。

A huge wave came and swallowed Nüwa. She never came out again.

又是一阵巨浪拍来，勇敢的女娃被海浪吞没了，再也没上来。

Day broke and the sun rose. Nüwa had become a small bird
flying in the sky.

这时,天已黎明,鲜红的太阳冉冉升起。女娃死后变成了一只小鸟在霞
光中翔翔。

"Jingwei!" "Jingwei!" the bird shouted. People then called this little bird Jingwei.

这小鸟在飞时不停地叫着"精卫"、"精卫",人们就把小鸟叫做精卫鸟。

Every day, Jingwei would carry some small twigs and stones from the West Mountain and throw them into the East Sea. She was determined to fill the sea so that the Sea Dragon King wouldn't be able to hurt anyone else again.

精卫鸟每天从西山衔些小树枝和小石子,投到东海里。她立志要将大海填平,不让海龙王再害别人。

All year round, no matter whether it was sunny or cloudy, windy or rainy, she never stopped throwing stones into the sea.

一年四季，不管是天阴天晴，还是刮风下雨，它从不间断地向大海投着小石子。

"Forget it, little girl," said the Sun to Jingwei. "How can you possibly fill the vast sea with these little stones?"

太阳公公心疼地对精卫说:"算了吧,孩子,你衔来的小石子怎能填平浩瀚的大海呢!"

"Even though the sea is big, it becomes smaller every time I throw stones into it," answered Jingwei determinedly. "I'm sure the sea will be filled with stones some day."

　　精卫坚定地说:"大海再大,我填一点,它就小一点,总有一天会填平的。"

The Sea overheard their conversation. Said he, "don't imagine you can fill me with those stones even in a million years!"

他们的对话被大海听到了，大海冷笑说："小鸟儿，你填一百万年也休想把我填平。"

"If one million years are not long enough, I'll spend ten million or even a hundred million years to fill you with the stones!" said Jingwei firmly.

精卫坚决回答:"一百万年不行,我就填一千万年,哪怕填一万万年,我也要把你填平!"

Later Jingwei got married to a seagull and gave birth to a great many little birds.

传说后来精卫与海燕结婚了，生下许多小鸟。

The boys were all like their father, flying bravely through storms.

生下的雄鸟像海燕，它们像父亲那样勇敢地在暴风中翱翔。

The girls were all like their mother. They never stopped throwing stones into the sea.

生下的雌鸟像精卫，它们像妈妈那样不停地衔着小石子扔进大海。

Thousands of years have passed. Today the Jingwei birds are still working very hard, throwing twigs and stones into the sea. How brave and strong-willed they are!

多少万年过去了，据说精卫鸟一直每天都在向大海里扔着小树枝和小石子。她们是多么的顽强和有毅力啊！